Little Bridge Farm

Oscar's New Friends

Oscar the pony is only little, but his life is about to change in a *big* way. There are lots of animals to meet at his new home, but will they all be friends...?

Look out for all the Little Bridge Farm books!

Oscar's New Friends

Smudge Finds the Trail

Tiger's Great Adventure

Dilly Saves the Day

Little Bridge Farm

Oscar's New Friends

PETER CLOVER

Illustrated by Angela Swan

■ SCHOLASTIC

First published in 2007 by Scholastic Children's Books
An imprint of Scholastic Ltd
Euston House, 24 Eversholt Street
London, NW1 1DB, UK
Registered office: Westfield Road, Southam, Warwickshire, CV47 0RA
SCHOLASTIC and associated logos are trademarks and/or registered
trademarks of Scholastic Inc.

10 digit ISBN 0 439 95097 X
13 digit ISBN 978 0439 95097 8

British Library Cataloguing-in-Publication Data
A CIP catalogue record for this book is available from the British Library

Printed in the UK by CPI Bookmarque, Croydon, CR0 4TD
Papers used by Scholastic Children's Books are made from wood grown in
sustainable forests.

3 5 7 9 10 8 6 4 2

This is a work of fiction. Names, characters, places, incidents and dialogues are
products of the author's imagination or are used fictitiously. Any resemblance
to actual people, living or dead, events or locales is entirely coincidental.

www.scholastic.co.uk/zone

To Stephen and Missy Blue

Chapter One

Little Bridge Farm was bathed in golden light as the setting sun disappeared slowly behind Great Oak Hill.

Oscar – a young chestnut pony – glanced nervously at the Big Red Barn. Then he looked around at the empty meadows. Beyond the farmhouse, he could see a dark forest and green rolling hills. It was all new to him. He looked back at Suzy, his very best friend, and blew a desperate whinny.

Suzy threw her arms around Oscar's neck and gave him one last goodbye

1

hug. Oscar knew that Suzy was trying to be brave for his sake, but he could still hear her snuffles as she struggled not to cry. Suzy and Oscar had always been best friends and now he was saying goodbye to her – for ever.

Oscar nudged his velvet muzzle against Suzy's cheek and whickered softly. Then he looked up and saw the tears rolling down her face.

Oscar whinnied sadly.

Suzy rubbed her eyes and sobbed. "I hope you'll be happy here, Oscar. Farmer Rob is a very nice man. And I know he'll look after you really well."

Oscar gazed down at the ground. Suzy wouldn't be able to visit him any more. She used to visit him three days a week at the Big City Stables. Suzy had explained to Oscar that her family was moving away. Her dad had been given an important job abroad, and they couldn't take a pony with them. Oscar knew Suzy would find him a good new home, but his heart still ached at the thought of saying goodbye.

Farmer Rob Newberry gently took hold of Oscar's halter as Suzy's mum led her away to the waiting car.

Oscar neighed sadly. His ears lay flat against his head as he pawed the soft earth with his hooves.

"I'll always love you," called Suzy.

And I'll never forget you, Oscar thought, as he whickered a last goodbye. Giant tears rolled from the pony's eyes. Even though Oscar wasn't a baby any more, he was still very young, and he had never felt so frightened or lonely in his entire life. He watched the family car drive slowly away, over the little stone bridge, back to the Big City. And his heart broke.

"Goodbye, Suzy," he said, as the car turned a corner and disappeared for ever.

Oscar looked up at the sky. The moon was coming out from behind some clouds, but it was very dark here in the countryside.

Where are all the bright lights? he thought.

It was very quiet as well. Not like the Big City. He was used to hearing cars whizzing along all night. But then there was something – a strange hooting sound Oscar had never heard before. The little pony pricked up his ears.

"What was that?" Oscar snorted. He felt a bit scared.

"Steady, young fella," said Farmer Rob soothingly. He rubbed Oscar's neck.

Oscar looked around nervously as Farmer Rob led him by his halter rope.

Farmer Rob stopped at the Big Red Barn and swung open the huge wooden doors. Oscar gave a little swallow and looked inside. This barn was enormous. And it was very dark and spooky!

The farmer flicked on the light switch and filled the barn with a soft, amber glow. Wooden beams and criss-crossed rafters held up the vast roof which towered above Oscar's head. He looked up, feeling dizzy. Oscar had never been inside such a huge, roomy place before. His stable in the Big City had been quite small. And a little cramped. Oscar used to share his stall with haughty Harriet, a thoroughbred hunter.

At the end of the big barn was a row of four wooden stalls. Oscar could see that there were other animals inside three of them: two great big ones, and a scrawny,

scrappy one.

Oscar hesitated. He placed one foot gingerly on the sawdust which covered the floor. But then Farmer Rob clapped him lightly on the rump, and Oscar trotted inside his new, empty stall.

"There you are, Oscar," said the farmer. "That wasn't too bad, was it?"

Oscar hadn't decided yet. He shook out his mane and tried to look at the animals in the other stalls. Although he couldn't see them clearly, he was almost certain that they were squinting back at him. Oscar hoped they would be friendlier than the snooty Big City ponies – especially haughty Harriet.

Oscar felt the warmth of the barn through his thick, chestnut coat. Then he spotted something in the corner. It was a mother dog with her tiny, newborn puppies snuggling up against her pink belly. They all looked so happy

together and Oscar felt himself slowly relax.

Perhaps I could be happy here, too, he thought.

There was a small side window in the stall where Oscar could see out across the farmyard. Sweet-smelling hay hung in a net. A corner trough was filled with fresh water. And a nice, crunchy swede dangled temptingly from a string.

"Don't worry, boy. You'll soon settle in." The farmer smiled. Then he shut the stall gate, flicked off the lights and closed the barn door. Silver moonlight filtered through Oscar's window and lit the stall with an eerie glow.

At first the barn was quiet. Oscar tilted his head and listened to the silence around him. He could hear shuffling straw. Something huffed and made a nervous chewing noise. Then there was the sound of a bolt sliding across a wooden stall-gate. Oscar realized that one of the other animals must have let itself out of its stall!

Oscar wondered what kind of animal it could possibly be. Were they coming over to get a better look at him? His legs started to tremble. Whoever it was, Oscar hoped it would be a friend. Oscar needed all the new friends he could find.

He shut his eyes tightly. And waited.

Chapter Two

"H-h-hello," stammered a thin, stringy voice.

Oscar opened his eyes, to see a strange creature peering at him over the stall's wooden gate. In the moonlight it looked really spooky. Oscar had never seen anything quite like this animal before.

"H-h-hello." The creature spoke again. It was silver-grey and hairy with a thin face, funny green eyes, a straggly beard and two horns on the top of its head.

"Hello," said Oscar, trying to sound friendly and not too frightened. "I'm new here and my name is Oscar. . . What kind of animal are you?"

"I'm a mountain goat and my name's F-F-Filbert," stammered the hairy creature.

"What's a mountain?" asked Oscar.

"It's like a very b-b-big hill," said Filbert. "Only b-b-bigger."

Then he sprung his forelegs on top of the stall's wooden gate and stretched his neck out to snaffle Oscar's juicy swede.

"FILBERT!" boomed a deep, commanding voice from the neighbouring stall. "Have you forgotten *all* of your manners?"

Oscar's eyes had finally grown accustomed to the moonlit glow of the barn. He saw that the deep, booming voice belonged to a giant horse in the very next stall.

Crunch, crunch, crunch. The swede disappeared.

"S-s-sorry, sorry, sorry," said Filbert, licking his lips. "It's just that they don't feed me here. They never, ever feed me here!"

"FILBERT!" the same voice boomed again. "You know that's simply not true."

"You must forgive him, Oscar," said a second, gentler voice.

Oscar stretched his neck and saw that the voice came from another giant horse in the furthest stall at the end.

"Farmer Rob feeds Filbert three times a day. But he's always hungry."

"I'm s-s-starved, starved, starved," insisted Filbert. He curled back his top lip and tried to eat Oscar's tail.

"FILBERT!" boomed the giant horse again. "Stop that at once."

The scrappy goat lowered his head sulkily, and nibbled on his hooves.

"We're terribly sorry about that," said the gentler voice.

Oscar smiled as he peered over the side of his stall at the two big horses. They were both enormous. Oscar had never seen such gigantic horses before. They made him feel tiny.

"My name is Duke," said the bigger of the two.

"And I'm Daisy," whinnied the gentle mare. "We're both shire horses."

Duke was dappled grey with a long, black mane and matching tail. Daisy was the golden colour of honey with a white blaze on her forehead. Oscar thought she was beautiful.

"Welcome to Little Bridge Farm," whickered Duke.

"And welcome to Big Red Barn!" Daisy smiled.

"It's very nice to meet you," said Oscar. "I've just lost my best friend, and I don't really know anyone here."

Filbert stuck his head through a gap in Oscar's stall.

"You know, know, know me!" He grinned.

Oscar was feeling a lot more relaxed now. He swished his tail and puffed out his proud chest, trying to make himself as big as the shire horses. It was nice to talk and make new friends. His old neighbours at the Big City Stables didn't talk much at all. They just looked down their long, thoroughbred noses and snickered when Oscar tried to make conversation.

Duke and Daisy weren't like that. They told Oscar all about Little Bridge Farm.

"Most of the animals here have been rescued," said Daisy.

"Or they came here because there was nowhere else for them to go," added Duke.

That made Oscar feel sad and lonely again. He thought of Suzy and a little flutter danced in his stomach.

"I'm here," interrupted Filbert, "because . . . because . . . because. . . . Oh, I've forgotten again!"

Oscar smiled at the silly goat, and realized that his nervous butterflies had suddenly vanished.

"Farmer Rob Newberry and his family look after us all," said Daisy. "You'll meet the children in the morning when they bring us and all the other animals breakfast."

Filbert's head popped back through the gap in Oscar's stall.

"I hope they b-b-bring me breakfast," he stammered. "They n-n-never bring me any breakfast."

"FILBERT!"

"S-s-sorry!"

Oscar laughed. He had a feeling he was going to like it here at Little Bridge Farm. He only hoped that all the other animals would like him as well!

Duke and Daisy smiled and yawned. It had been a long day.

"We'll introduce you to everyone in the morning," said Duke. "Now say goodnight, Filbert."

"Goodnight F-F-Filbert."

"Very funny," boomed Duke.

Oscar chuckled to himself. Haughty Harriet never made jokes. Except about Oscar!

"Sleep well," said Daisy, kindly.

Duke and Daisy were soon snoring peacefully. And Filbert was snuffling in his dreams – probably eating a giant haystack. The little puppies were sleeping soundly in the corner, curled up snugly in their mother's fur.

Oscar closed his eyes and tried to relax, but now that everyone else had gone to sleep, he noticed that there were lots of strange noises in the barn. He could hear odd creaks and funny groans as the wooden beams settled for the night. Oscar's ears twitched at every click and creak. He missed the sleepy drone of the Big City cars. But he didn't miss haughty Harriet snoring in his ear.

It was no good. He was wide awake. He turned to peer through the window in his stall. The moon smiled at Oscar through his little window. And while Little Bridge Farm slept peacefully, Oscar stayed awake, and waited to see what the morning would bring.

Chapter Three

A burst of brilliant sunshine streamed through Oscar's window. There were fresh animal smells and noises all around him. Outside the barn, Oscar could see cows who had come into the farmyard from the fields. They were mooing lazily and scraping their feet on the cobblestones as they formed a noisy queue by the milking parlour.

The sheep were busy gossiping in their pens while their baby lambs played "king of the castle" by jumping on and off the top of a grassy mound in the middle of the pen. Pigs grunted and snuffled happily in their sty, ignoring the plump pink piglets who pulled playfully at their corkscrew tails. And chickens clucked noisily from their roost in the maple tree. As Oscar watched, a big, black cockerel crowed the hour.

Oscar recognized all the animals from a Big City farm he'd once visited with Suzy. He shook out his chestnut mane and neighed happily at the memory.

Little Bridge Farm was wide awake, and so was Oscar.

Suddenly, the big doors swung open and the barn was flooded with glorious sunlight. Oscar blinked at the sudden brightness. Then he gasped as he saw two children walking towards him.

"The boy, that's Ethan Newberry," whinnied Duke.

"And the girl," said Daisy, "her name is Rosie."

At first, Oscar thought that he was seeing things. From a distance, Rosie looked exactly like Suzy. But when she got closer, Oscar could see that Rosie's hair was red and she had a lot more freckles.

Ethan and Rosie strolled up to the stalls. Oscar puffed out his chest and flicked up his ears.

"Hello, Oscar," said Rosie.

Oscar blew a friendly snort. Then he saw the juicy apple Rosie held in her outstretched palm.

"An apple. An apple. She's g-g-got an apple." Filbert was so excited that he almost tripped himself up.

"Here you are, Oscar," said Rosie. "A lovely morning treat for you."

Ethan reached over the stall gate and ruffled Oscar's silky mane.

Filbert watched closely as Oscar munched on the apple. Oscar licked his lips. It was delicious.

"You're a real beauty," said Ethan.
"This is the first time Rosie and I have
had a pony."

Rosie stroked Oscar's face while
Filbert skittered around on his skinny
legs, hoping for an apple of his own.

Rosie and Ethan went to the feed bins and scooped portions into four different buckets. One bucket went to Oscar. One to Duke. One to Daisy. And one to Filbert.

"You see," whinnied Daisy. "Filbert told you they never feed him!"

"Do we get fed by the same children every day?" asked Oscar.

Daisy nodded.

Oscar thought that was *really* nice! Suzy was only able to feed him on the days she visited.

While he tucked into his breakfast, Rosie and Ethan set out all the feeds for the other animals.

Oscar looked up from his bucket as Lucy, the farmer's wife, came into the barn. Oscar knew who she was because Rosie and Ethan introduced her to him. "Meet our mum!" they said, pulling her over to Oscar's stall. She had dark, curly hair which bounced around her shoulders and a bright, happy smile.

"So this is the handsome new arrival I've heard so much about!" she said in a jolly voice. "Come on, Oscar. Let's get you outside into the fresh air." Lucy patted Oscar's neck and led him by his halter out into the golden morning.

"See you later," whinnied Duke and Daisy.

Outside, Oscar took his first good look around at the rest of the farm. It all looked quite different in the daylight.

Opposite Big Red Barn was the farmhouse, White Flower Cottage. Pink and white roses climbed over the large front porch. Oscar saw a big, fat tabby cat curled up asleep on the porch's swing-seat. Bumblebees buzzed and hummed busily among the brightly coloured flower beds.

Oscar sighed contentedly. He breathed in the fresh smell of flowers as he walked with Lucy. Then his ears flattened against his head.

"What is it, boy?" asked Lucy. "What's wrong?"

Oscar had stopped suddenly and was staring at a small river, bubbling its way past the house and behind the barn.

"It's only Willow River," said Lucy. "Have you never seen a river before?" She smoothed Oscar's face and gently stroked his muzzle as he shook his head.

She was right! Oscar had never, EVER seen a river before. There were no rivers in the Big City.

Oscar took a good look. Now that he had a chance to study it properly, he could see that the clear, rushing water was really beautiful.

He felt a bit silly. But he walked on through the rest of the farmyard with a

26

spring in his step, his head held high and his long tail swishing.

Lucy opened the gate in a white-railed fence, and led Oscar into the most fantastic field he had ever seen in his life. The grass was velvet green and a hill rose out of the middle of the field. At the top of the hill was a giant oak tree and behind the field were more hills and an emerald forest of tall trees. Oscar couldn't wait to run all the way up to the oak tree at the top of that hill – what fun!

"Off you go, boy," said Lucy, as she turned Oscar out into the field.

Oscar could hardly believe it as he stepped cautiously on to the soft grass. It was very different from what he was used to. He had never seen so much green before. This was so much bigger than City Park where Suzy used to take him riding.

Can all this really be for me? Oscar

thought. He was so excited that he galloped round the field, kicking up his heels. Then he raced up to the top of the hill as fast as he could.

In the shade of the giant oak tree at the top of Great Oak Hill, Oscar lowered his head and nibbled the sweet, green grass.

This is the best grass I've ever tasted, thought Oscar as he closed his eyes, dreamily. He was so content that he began to feel very sleepy.

He shook out his mane and went to look for a nice shady spot to have a nap. He went to stand in the cool shade of the giant oak.

Very soon, Oscar was lost in a dream of green rolling hills and softly gurgling rivers.

Chapter Four

Oscar was enjoying his dream when he was rudely awakened by a sharp peck on his ear.

"Ow!" He leapt up on to his hooves in an instant. "Who did that?" Then he glanced around looking for whatever it was that had attacked him.

A strange honking noise made Oscar look down. Waddling around the bottom of the giant oak tree, squawking and flapping, was a very fat, white goose. He seemed to be upset about something.

"Oh, my, my, my. Squash! Squash!

Squash!" honked the goose. He shook out his feathers in alarm as Oscar cocked his head to one side, trying to make out what the goose was saying.

"My, my, my. All squashed. All squashed," said the goose, over and over again. He stamped his webbed feet and pointed with a wing to the exact spot where Oscar had been lying.

"Are you OK?" asked Oscar politely. He was puzzled by this strange behaviour.

The goose took a deep breath, dramatically placed its other wing over its eyes, and fainted.

"Oh dear!" said Oscar, not quite knowing what to do. He lowered his head and nudged the goose gently with his soft muzzle.

"HONK!" The goose suddenly shot up into the air. Oscar nearly jumped right out of his horseshoes.

"Monty, Monty, Monty," honked the goose, who was now running around in circles. "You've squashed my best friend, Monty the moorhen. You rolled over and squashed him in your sleep!"

Oscar looked down to where the crazy bird was pointing. Oscar's heart thumped loudly in his chest as he started to understand what the goose was trying to tell him. There was a cluster of black and white feathers on the grass – just where he'd been sleeping.

"Oh, no!" Oscar gasped. How could he have been so clumsy? "I'm so s-s-sorry," he stammered. "It was an accident. I didn't mean to hurt your friend."

"You've flattened him like a pancake," hissed the goose. Only this time, the fat bird seemed to be smiling. "Flat as a pancake!"

Oscar was about to apologize again, when suddenly, the goose burst into fits of laughter.

"Funny. Funny. Funny! It's *so* funny," said the goose, giggling. Then he fell on to his back and paddled his legs in the air.

Oscar stared at the bird in disbelief.

"My name is Ernest." The fat goose chuckled as he struggled back on to his feet, smoothing his ruffled feathers. "And my friend, Monty the moorhen, is. . ."

"HERE!" A cheeky little moorhen jumped out from its hiding place behind the tree and ran in circles around Oscar's legs.

Ernest the goose began laughing again as Monty flew on to Oscar's back. Oscar could feel him run all the way up his neck, and perch himself on top of his head. The bird's feet tickled in Oscar's mane.

"We played a trick. We played a trick," sang Monty from his pony perch.

Oscar craned round and almost went cross-eyed peering up at the moorhen.

"It's a tradition," explained Ernest. "Here at Little Bridge Farm, we always welcome the newcomers by playing a trick."

"And that was a GREAT trick," said Monty. "One of the best! Did you like it?"

Oscar started laughing. It really *was* quite a funny joke. And he was so pleased that he hadn't actually squashed anyone.

Monty slid back down Oscar's neck with his skinny legs in the air, and hopped off on to the ground.

Ernest and Monty laughed and then turned to face . . . an enormous grey and white, shaggy dog.

The dog glared at the two birds, then looked kindly at Oscar.

"May I introduce myself?" he said,

politely. "My name is Trumpet. Welcome to Little Bridge Farm."

Oscar suddenly felt a bit shy. Trumpet looked very important.

"And as for you two," said the big dog, turning his attention back to Ernest and Monty. "Your tricks and jokes will get the better of you one day!"

Oscar couldn't help staring. He looked Trumpet up and down.

"You look a bit like a sheep," he said, timidly, trying not to sound rude. "You're very big and woolly!"

"I'm an Old English sheepdog," said Trumpet, proudly. "I'm supposed to look like this!"

Just then, a tiny white dog came yapping up the hill towards them. The little Jack Russell skidded on the slippery grass and crashed into Trumpet. Trumpet hardly moved. The tiny dog bounced off and lay on her back, kicking her legs and panting for breath.

"May I also introduce Parsley," said Trumpet with an affectionate sigh, looking down at the tiny dog.

Parsley leapt to her feet, wagging her tail furiously. She was so excited she couldn't speak.

Oscar smiled and felt all warm inside as Parsley took a deep breath and gave herself the hiccups.

"I believe it's almost lunch time," said Trumpet. "Why don't we all go down together?"

Oscar had to admit that he was quite hungry. And he couldn't have felt happier as he strolled down the hill with his new friends on either side.

"We tricked him! We tricked him!" whistled Monty.

Oscar flicked his tail and smiled to himself. Parsley ran circles round and round his legs as he walked. It was fun living here at Little Bridge Farm.

Chapter Five

Oscar stood at the gate and waited patiently as Ethan and Rosie Newberry filled his dinner pail with pony nuts and topped up his trough with fresh water.

Ernest and Monty had gone for a swim. Trumpet and Parsley were sharing a bone, leaving Oscar, for the moment, all alone. Oscar pushed his nose into the bucket and gobbled up his bran nuts. Mmmmmmm. They were very tasty. He was just sipping at the water when he felt something soft and wet licking at his ankles.

Oscar's eyes opened wide as he peered

back through his own legs. And there, in his shadow, was a cute little puppy.

"Hi!" squealed the puppy, excitedly. "My name's Smudge. And I'm a Labrador. What's your name?"

Smudge wagged his tail as he scampered out from beneath the pony.

"My name is Oscar."

"Oscar? That's a nice name," yapped Smudge cheerfully. "You're new here, aren't you?"

Oscar was just about to answer when the little puppy burst out with his own story.

"I was rescued by Ethan Newberry," said Smudge. "I was abandoned, but I don't remember my other home. Now I live *here* at Little Bridge Farm. It's *brilliant!*"

The little puppy was so cute and bouncy that Oscar couldn't resist nuzzling the top of his head with his soft muzzle, and nibbling at his perky ears.

"It'll soon be story time," announced Smudge. "Old Spotty the pig always tells a story after lunch."

Oscar pricked up his ears. He loved stories. "Can I come with you and listen to Old Spotty's stories?" he asked. "Will it be OK?"

"Of course," said Smudge. "Everyone's welcome. Especially newcomers like you. Follow me!"

Oscar went to stand at the edge of the field, eager to hear the stories. Five fluffy ducklings clustered around his hooves. Oscar stood very still – he was afraid of stepping on them!

"These are some of my friends," said Smudge. "And this is Oscar, everyone."

The ducklings peeped excitedly.

"Are you the newcomer?"

"Did you really live in the Big City?"

"What was it like?"

"Why did you come to Little Bridge Farm?"

The questions came all at once. Oscar hardly had time to answer the first question when Amber's puppies from the Big Red Barn suddenly surrounded him.

"Hello, Oscar." All six puppies greeted the pony together. They recognized him from the barn. "Have you met the wild kittens yet?"

Oscar shook his head slowly and looked around, but the kittens were shy and crouched low in the long grass. Only their glinting eyes, pointy ears and swishing tails were visible as they peered at Oscar nervously.

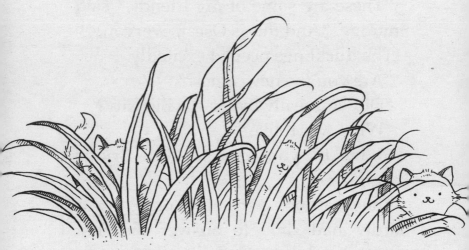

Suddenly, Old Spotty, the storyteller, walked into the field. Old Spotty was an enormous black and white spotted pig with wobbly cheeks and a belly that almost touched the floor. She waddled slowly to the front of the field.

Old Spotty's three noisy grand-piglets squealed and squeaked as they followed the big sow to the shade of the Telling Tree.

A very young foal left its mother's side, and tottered on long, shaky legs to listen to Old Spotty's stories, too. But when the foal saw Oscar standing by the fence, with all the younger animals gathered around him, he changed direction and gambolled across to Oscar for a closer look.

Old Spotty could see that something was going on. Oscar watched her amble over to investigate.

"What time did you arrive?" asked one of the baby ducklings.

"What was your journey like?"

"How far did you come?"

"Was the Big City scary?"

Oscar laughed. There were so many questions from all the youngsters. He simply didn't know which one to answer first. Even the wild kittens overcame their fear of the newcomer and clambered over each other as they crept forward to listen.

"Well . . . I used to belong to a girl called Suzy," began Oscar. "I shared a stable with lots of other ponies."

Old Spotty's grand-piglets oinked their way to the front of the group with more questions.

"How many ponies?"

"What were they like?"

Soon Oscar was so busy telling his story that he failed to notice Old Spotty huffing and puffing her way through the youngsters.

"Yes," exclaimed Old Spotty. "That reminds me of a time when I. . ."

"Did you have lots and lots of friends?" One of the youngsters interrupted the old sow.

"There were lots of horses and ponies at the stables," answered Oscar, brightly. "But I didn't really have many friends. The Big City ponies were all very snooty and didn't talk very much."

Old Spotty tried again. "Yes, yes. I'm sure that's very interesting. Anyway, that also reminds me of a. . ."

"Tell us about the other ponies," whinnied the baby foal.

Old Spotty huffed a noisy snort and waddled her way to the other side of the gathering to get closer. Her cheeks were turning very pink. And her brows were beginning to set into a heavy frown. In fact, Oscar thought she was looking quite cross!

Chapter Six

Old Spotty stood next to Oscar and cleared her throat with a loud cough.

"I shall be telling *my* story very soon," she announced. "So, if everyone would like to make their way to the Telling Tree!"

Nobody seemed to hear Old Spotty. Everyone was more interested in asking Oscar questions.

"What was it like being looked after by different people every day?" asked little Smudge.

Old Spotty was hopping from one foot to another. She seemed to be getting very impatient. Finally, the grumpy old sow shook her head from side to side. Large, leathery ears flapped themselves against her fat cheeks making a loud slapping sound. All the youngsters instantly fell silent.

"Am I going to be allowed to tell my story or not!" she exclaimed, crossly.

Oscar stopped speaking and looked up, startled. Old Spotty was clearly very annoyed about something! She stomped her trotters into the earth and glared fiercely up at Oscar.

Oscar smiled.

Old Spotty didn't.

She trembled with anger and puffed herself out to her full size.

"You are a very rude, ill-mannered newcomer," she announced in a loud voice. "The young ones come here every day to listen to *my* stories."

Oscar suddenly felt embarrassed. Everyone was staring at him.

"You are an outsider," oinked Old Spotty, "and you don't understand the way things work at Little Bridge Farm." She drew in a deep breath. "You don't belong here!" the pig announced. Then she waddled off, huffing and puffing like an old train, with her huge body swaying and her tail twitching.

All the little ones followed her in silence, and sat quietly beneath the Telling Tree. Oscar was left completely alone. He didn't know what to say or do! Oscar hadn't meant to hurt anyone's feelings, but he had made Old Spotty very angry.

Oscar stood by the fence with his head hanging low. Was Old Spolly right? Perhaps he didn't belong here after all!

When he lived in the Big City, Suzy's visits always made him feel better if he was lonely. Oscar wished Suzy would come to see him now. But he knew she wouldn't. She was too far away.

"Cheer up, Oscar." Trumpet's friendly voice made the little pony look up.

"I can't," replied Oscar, sadly. "I didn't mean to . . . but I've upset Old Spotty. She's really cross with me." Oscar told Trumpet all about what had happened.

Trumpet listened carefully. Oscar could see that the dog must be very wise and waited to see what he would say.

"If I were you," began Trumpet, "I would let things settle down overnight. Try to talk with Old Spotty first thing in the morning. She will have calmed down by then. Her bark is a lot worse than her bite, you know! Or should I say her *oink*?"

Oscar nodded, but he couldn't help feeling like he had just ruined everything on his first day at Little Bridge Farm.

Chapter Seven

The sun was going down and grey storm clouds rolled in from the hills as Farmer Rob led Oscar out of the field and back to the Big Red Barn. After he had spoken to Trumpet, Oscar had been alone all afternoon with lots of time to think about how he had upset Old Spotty.

He was feeling really miserable. Now all he wanted to do was snuggle up in his cosy stall and sleep. With a pat on Oscar's rump, Farmer Rob left him to step into his wooden pen. But once

Oscar was inside, he found a horrible surprise waiting for him.

Oscar couldn't believe his eyes. All his lovely, soft, sweet-smelling straw had gone. *Perhaps Farmer Rob doesn't want me either?* he thought, looking around. But Farmer Rob had already gone.

Oscar lowered his head, sadly, and wondered if he should ask his friends Daisy and Duke about it. But he could

hear gentle snoring coming from the giant shire horses' stall. He whispered to Filbert, but there was no answer.

Oscar felt very alone as he stood quietly in his cold, empty stall with no soft straw to lie down on.

It's true, thought Oscar, sadly. *Everything that Old Spotty said is true. I don't belong here.*

Oscar felt a salty tear trickle from his eye.

"If I'm not wanted at Little Bridge Farm," Oscar said quietly to himself, "then there's only one thing left I can do." He decided that he must try and make his way back to the Big City and his old home at the Big City stables.

Farmer Rob had left the barn doors open slightly, to allow the cool evening breeze to circulate. Oscar arched his neck over the stall's gate and pulled the bolt across with his teeth. He hesitated for a brief moment and looked around. The Big Red Barn had almost been home.

Oscar thought he had made lots of new friends here. But he had been wrong. Now it was time to leave.

Quietly, Oscar made his way past the sleeping puppies to the open barn doors. Then he stepped outside into the moonlit yard. Overhead the sky was black and thick with cloud.

As he passed the maple tree he saw the roosting hens settled on their bedtime branches. No one stirred as he gently pushed open the farm gates and began his journey back over the little stone bridge.

Willow River bubbled and rushed beneath the bridge as Oscar glanced back at the farm for the last time. He noticed the pretty apple orchard.

Mmmmm, he thought, sadly. *It would have been nice to have snaffled a few rosy apples from there one day!* Apples had always been one of Oscar's favourite treats.

The pony sniffed back another tear, then glanced up at the sky and shivered. The air had suddenly turned cold. Big black clouds had covered the bright moon. Oscar raised his muzzle and sniffed. There was rain in the air. The little pony felt frightened as he quickened his pace and trotted down the road away from the farm.

It wasn't long before he came to a crossroads. Oscar looked one way and then the other.

Which way? he thought.

In the distance, a deep roll of thunder rumbled down from the skies. A storm was coming. Oscar quickly made a decision and turned right, following the course of the river as it rushed behind a bank of thick trees lining the road.

From the forest, an owl hooted, and the first drops of rain splashed on to Oscar's face.

Oscar hunched his shoulders and walked down the road, sheltering beneath the trees. The rain became heavier, sploshing into the puddles at Oscar's feet. His mane was soaking wet and matted against his neck.

Suddenly, Oscar pricked up his ears. Through the drumming rain he heard a familiar sound. It was the sound of a dog yapping frantically. It was the sound of a dog in a lot of trouble. And it was coming from the river bank, just below the trees where Oscar was standing.

Oscar hurried to investigate. Lightning suddenly flashed and filled the night sky with a brilliant white light. Oscar gasped at the scene lit up before him. Parsley, the little Jack Russell, was standing on the far bank calling for help. And there, in the middle of Willow River, were three of Old Spotty's grand-piglets, slowly being pulled downstream!

Chapter Eight

Parsley was in a terrible state. She didn't know which way to turn. When she saw Oscar standing on the opposite bank, she barked and yapped at the top of her voice for help.

"Help!" she called. "I can't reach them!"

Oscar could see that poor Parsley had been trying to pull the piglets out and drag them to the safety of the bank. But she was far too small and the bank was far too slippery.

The piglets were squealing with fright

and slowly being pulled by the current downstream into deeper water. The rain lashed down as they paddled their little legs and tried to swim, but the river was flowing so quickly and the piglets were exhausted.

Without stopping to think, Oscar picked his way carefully down the bank. His hooves slid in the mud as he waded into the rushing water.

"Don't worry. I'm coming!"

Oscar gently caught hold of the first little piglet with his mouth. He lifted the piglet by the scruff of her neck and placed her safely on to the bank.

"Thank you," she panted, shivering in the wind and rain.

The second piglet was hanging on to some driftwood. "Help!" he called to Oscar.

The brave pony plucked him from the foaming river and placed him safely next to his sister. The third piglet was floundering in the water, struggling between the two banks.

Lightning flashed and the piglet squealed with fright as he bobbed beneath the water.

"I'm sorry," yapped Parsley. "It's all my fault." The little dog was really upset. She ran frantically to and fro on the bank as Oscar tried to catch the third piglet. The rain was making it difficult to see.

Finally, Oscar reached for the last piglet, who was thrashing and paddling wildly in the water. Oscar grabbed him by the scruff and delivered him to the bank. The piglets were all safe!

Then Oscar tried to climb up on to the bank himself. But suddenly, he found that he couldn't lift his legs! He had been far too busy rescuing Old Spotty's grand-piglets to notice that his own hooves had slowly begun to sink into the gooey mud on the river bed!

"Oh no," said Oscar. "I'm well and truly stuck!"

The rain poured off his mane, and the mud sucked at his feet. Oscar couldn't move. Worse than that, he could feel himself slowly sinking.

"I think I'm in BIG trouble," Oscar said.

Parsley didn't seem to notice what was happening. "Come on, Oscar," she called, shaking the rain from her coat. "Let's get out of here!"

But Oscar just stared straight ahead and tried not to move a muscle. "I can't, Parsley," he said. "I can't move! I'm stuck in the mud, and I'm sinking."

Parsley pricked up her ears. "Sinking? Oh, no! Not sinking! What shall I do?"

"Go for help," urged Oscar. "And FAST!"

Oscar watched through the downpour as the little dog tried to scrabble up the grassy bank. The piglets wanted to follow, but the rain had made the banks too wet and slippery. Each time they almost reached the top, they slipped and tumbled all the way back down. Parsley wasn't having much luck, either.

Lightning flashed again and the rain poured down. The piglets started crying. Parsley made one last attempt, but failed and tumbled back down the bank into the water.

Luckily, Oscar was just able to reach and fish her out. With a flick of his neck, Oscar gently tossed the little dog safely back to the shore. But the sudden movement disturbed the mud beneath Oscar's feet.

Parsley and the piglets watched in horror as Oscar's legs began to sink even deeper into the muddy water.

Poor Oscar was trembling with fright.

"We can't get up the bank," yapped Parsley, frantically. "What shall we do?"

Oscar had no idea.

Chapter Nine

Oscar lowered his head in despair. The rain had stopped, but the bank was still far too slippery for Parsley or the piglets to climb. They sat in silence with the trees dripping all around them.

Poor Oscar had never felt so miserable in all his life.

Suddenly he could hear voices coming from the direction of the farm road. Oscar flicked up his ears. Someone was up there! Oscar could hear two voices.

Parsley and the piglets heard them as well.

"Over here," they cried. "Help, help! We're over here!"

Oscar looked through the trees and saw Trumpet and Cider the cat bounding along the road.

"Trumpet! Cider! We're down here on the river bank!" Oscar called out as loudly as he could.

The two animals peered down at Oscar, standing in the river, up to his knees in mud.

"What's happened?" asked Trumpet. "Everyone's out looking for you. All the animals at the farm have been so worried. Filbert came back early from his nightly raid of the feed bins and realized that you were missing. He raised the alarm." Trumpet paused for breath. Then he caught sight of Parsley. "And what are YOU doing here, in the middle of the night with Old Spotty's grand-piglets?"

"This is all my fault," confessed the little dog straight away. "I sneaked the piglets out for a midnight adventure," Parsley said, guiltily. "We started playing a game of dares to see who could go out furthest into the river. But it all went horribly wrong." Poor Parsley was nearly in tears. "Oscar saved the piglets from drowning. But now he's stuck and in terrible danger. And it's all my fault!" Parsley slumped on to the wet grass and hid her face beneath her soggy paws.

Trumpet listened carefully to everything that Parsley told him. The big, woolly sheepdog slid down the bank and sniffed at the angry water swirling round Oscar's feet. He looked up again quickly.

"I'll stay here with Oscar. Cider – you go and fetch the other animals. Be as quick as you can. We don't have much time!"

The cat ran off. While she was gone, Trumpet turned to Oscar and asked, "Why did you leave the farm?"

"Well," began Oscar. "It all started when I spoiled Old Spotty's storytelling. I didn't mean to upset anyone but I ruined the afternoon. Then there was the straw. . ."

Trumpet looked dumbfounded. "The

straw? You'd better explain," the dog said, kindly.

"All my bedding was taken away," stammered Oscar. "On top of everything else, I thought that someone had taken the straw out of my stall as a way of telling me to go! It looked like no one wanted me at Little Bridge Farm, so I decided to leave. I thought it would be best for everybody."

"That's nonsense," said Trumpet. "Everyone at the farm really likes you, Oscar."

Oscar was very surprised. "But I thought—" he began.

"Well, you thought wrong," interrupted Trumpet. The big dog sniffed at the muddy water again, nervously. "Everyone's out looking for you because they were worried," he said. "Even Old Spotty. So let's stop all this foolishness and concentrate on getting you out of this mess!"

Oscar looked down at his hooves, buried in the sticky mud. How *was* he going to get out?

Then he saw Cider coming back down the road, followed by animals of all shapes and sizes. Everyone from Little Bridge Farm had come to help. There were cows and sheep, ducks and hens, horses and pigs, dogs and geese. Even Filbert the mountain goat was there, tottering about on the top of the bank, about to lose his balance.

"D-d-d-don't worry, Oscar. We'll save you."

Oscar looked up. Old Spotty was up there with Smudge, Ernest and Monty. Oscar smiled, awkwardly. Old Spotty called down. "Don't worry, Oscar. Everything will be all right."

Trumpet barked orders, and all the animals scurried around to gather leaves and dried grasses. They brought reeds from the river and dry bracken from the hedgerows. Then they carefully threw their matting on to the mud around Oscar's hooves.

Filbert was very light on his feet, and happily danced on top of the dried grasses, stamping it all into the mud. The animals brought more and more.

The dried bedding soon soaked up the squidgy mud. The smaller animals were light enough to step on to the surface and help Oscar lift his legs. The little pony was still stuck, but at least he wasn't sinking any more.

Then, Daisy and Duke appeared.

Daisy carried a coiled rope in her mouth, which she had brought from the farm. She held on to one end, and tossed the rope down to Trumpet.

"Pass the rope around Oscar's rump," she whinnied. "Then bring the other end back up here to Duke. Between us, we can use the rope as a sling!" It was a brilliant idea. The two giant shire horses would be able to pull Oscar free.

Filbert took the rope in his teeth and nimbly tiptoed his way across the grassy matting behind Oscar. Then he passed the rope back to Trumpet who bounded up the slippery bank to Duke. Duke took hold of the rope from Trumpet. Now the two shires each held one end of rope.

"Heave!" oinked Old Spotty. And the giant horses pulled. With a lot of squelching and heaving, Oscar was soon able to lift his legs clear.

"PULL!" called Old Spotty, as Daisy

and Duke dug in their hooves and hauled.

Everyone cheered as Oscar was pulled safely out of the river bed. He stepped on to the bank gratefully, with a big sigh of relief.

"Thank you, everyone," Oscar said.

"No – thank *you*!" yapped Parsley, excitedly. "You're a hero, Oscar. You saved Old Spotty's grand-piglets."

"Hurrah!" cheered all the animals. "Hurrah for Oscar!"

"And look around you at all your friends." Trumpet smiled. "They all came to help."

"You're all amazing," said Oscar, proudly. He felt a lump in his throat.

"Hurrah for Oscar," the animals cried over and over again, as they led him in a long procession back to Little Bridge Farm.

Chapter Ten

As Oscar nudged open the farm gates, Old Spotty sidled up next to him. She glanced up and cleared her throat.

"Ahhemmm!" The big sow looked rather embarrassed. Her face flushed a deep shade of pink. "I just wanted to say," she began, "that before we settle you back in ... you are very welcome at Little Bridge Farm. Perhaps I was a little hasty earlier this afternoon. And I'm sorry for those things I said that upset you."

Oscar felt his own face blush as he puffed out his chest, proudly.

"Thank you," said Oscar, softly. "And I'm sorry if *I* upset *you*. I only came to the field to listen to YOUR famous stories."

Old Spotty seemed flattered but looked away to hide it. Oscar smiled and raised his head high. Then he led everyone back into the farmyard.

All the animals stood in a circle around Oscar as Trumpet nudged Monty and Ernest to the front. The two birds looked very guilty about something, and stood looking down at their webbed feet.

"I think these two have something to say," announced Trumpet.

Ernest ruffled his feathers, awkwardly. "It seemed like a funny idea at the time," began the goose.

"We didn't realize that it would upset you so much, Oscar!" Monty the moorhen looked very uncomfortable. "We played such a good trick before. We thought this one was funnier!"

Poor Oscar didn't know what they were talking about.

"It was just another practical joke," said Ernest. "But it went terribly wrong!"

"We took your straw away," admitted

Monty. "And we're *very* sorry."

Oscar looked around at all the anxious faces peering at him.

Suddenly, Oscar laughed. "I suppose it was a funny thing to do."

"But not so funny that they should ever try anything so silly, ever again," said Trumpet.

"No. No. Never again. Never again," whistled Monty.

"So why don't we just forget everything," suggested Old Spotty. "And get all that lovely straw packed back into Oscar's stall?"

There was lots of fun, laughter and squawking as fresh, sweet-smelling straw was pulled from the neatly stacked bales and spread across the floor of Oscar's stall. At first, Daisy and Duke did most of the pulling with their big teeth, while Parsley, Trumpet, Ernest and Monty did most of the spreading. Old Spotty kept everyone organized. By the end, all the animals were helping.

Filbert was on lookout patrol, his head poking through a gap in the barn wall, where one of the wooden slats had slipped.

Suddenly, Filbert bleated a warning. "Q-q-quickly everyone," cried Filbert. "He's c-c-coming!"

The animals were making so much noise that Farmer Rob had woken up. And now he was coming over to Big Red Barn to investigate!

Oscar giggled as all the animals rushed back to their pens and stalls. He watched the chickens and geese dive through his open window. The ducks scrabbled under loose clapboards, and Oscar let out a breath as they escaped in the nick of time. Some animals hid behind straw bales or anywhere else they could find.

Only Filbert was having problems.

"I'm s-s-stuck," he stammered.

Silly Filbert's horns were stopping him from pulling his head back in through the gap in the boards.

"Oh, no. Oh, no. He's c-c-coming!" said Filbert, panicking.

Muffled laughter echoed around the

barn. Oscar was finding it very difficult not to giggle out loud!

Oscar pretended to close his eyes, but not all the way, so he could still see what was happening. Farmer Rob peeked around the door, and smiled to himself when he saw Filbert, half in and half out of the barn.

"I might have known it would be *you*, Filbert." Farmer Rob smiled as he took hold of the goat's horns and guided his head gently back through the hole. "Now let's get you back into your pen, you silly billy. I'm going to have to do something about that latch one day."

Farmer Rob closed Filbert's stall and locked the wooden gate. Then just before he left, he leant over the next stall and patted Oscar affectionately on the rump.

"Goodnight, boy," he whispered.

Oscar closed his eyes properly this time. He had never felt so happy.

A warm feeling spread and grew inside the little pony's heart.

As Farmer Rob quietly closed the barn doors, Oscar gave a contented sigh and fell fast asleep. Little Bridge Farm really was his home.

Look out for book two!

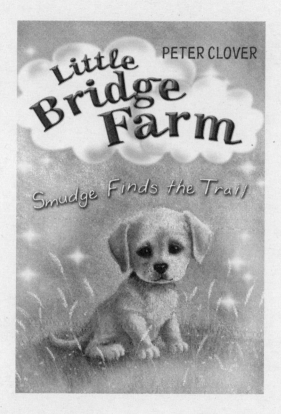

PETER CLOVER

Little Bridge Farm

Smudge Finds the Trail

Wheet-wheeeo!

Smudge watched as Trumpet streaked over to collect the straggling sheep.

Farmer Rob blew a series of further commands and Trumpet began to drive the sheep towards the pen, nipping gently at their heels.

Smudge barked and yapped loudly as he darted in and out of the big dog's legs, trying to help.

"What are we doing now?" asked Smudge.

Farmer Rob peeped his whistle.

"What does that mean?" asked Smudge.

Wheet. Wheet.

"Do we turn left? Or does that mean right?" Smudge had so many questions that poor Trumpet couldn't concentrate on what he was supposed to be doing.

One sheep broke free and ran all the way back down to the other end of the field.

Farmer Rob didn't look very pleased.

The sheep sniggered as Trumpet lifted Smudge gently by the scruff of his neck and dropped him softly back in the long grass at the edge of the field.

"I'm sorry, Smudge," said Trumpet. "But you're just getting in the way."

Smudge's tail drooped between his legs as he crept over to Ethan while Trumpet went back to doing his job.

Wheet-wheet. Whee-whooo. Farmer Rob's whistle blew again and Trumpet leapt into action. He quickly bounded down to collect the difficult sheep.

"Baa!" The three sheep gave in as Trumpet used all his years of experience and rounded them expertly into the wooden pen with the others. Then

Trumpet came over to Ethan and Smudge.

The little puppy peered up at the big dog and whimpered.

"It's no good," said Trumpet. "You're a Labrador retriever, *not* a sheepdog. You can't herd sheep. Rounding sheep is not what you are good at."

Ethan fondled Smudge's ears.

"But what *am* I good at?" asked Smudge. "If I can't herd sheep, what else can I do?"

Trumpet shook his head.

"You have to learn for yourself the thing that you are good at," he said, wisely.

Poor Smudge felt very sad as he left Ethan and wandered away from the field. Smudge sniffed at the ground and followed Parsley's scent back to the farm.

Don't miss the rest of the series!

PETER CLOVER

Little Bridge Farm

Tiger's Great Adventure